Sea Glass Summer

To Ann Mack, for showing me the ways of Maine
M. H.

To Sasha Brodsky
B. I.

~

Text copyright © 2019 by Michelle Houts
Illustrations copyright © 2019 by Bagram Ibatoulline

First edition 2019

Library of Congress Catalog Card Number pending
ISBN 978-0-7636-8443-3

19 20 21 22 23 24 CCP 10 9 8 7 6 5 4 3 2 1

Printed in Shenzhen, Guangdong, China

This book was typeset in Dante.
The illustrations were done in watercolor.

Candlewick Press
99 Dover Street
Somerville, Massachusetts 02144

visit us at www.candlewick.com

Sea Glass Summer

Michelle Houts

illustrated by Bagram Ibatoulline

CANDLEWICK PRESS

Some years ago, a boy named Thomas spent the summer at his grandmother's island cottage.

Early one morning, Thomas's grandmother gave him a magnifying glass.

"This belonged to your grandfather," she said.

Thomas liked the way the magnifying glass made every grain of sand look as big as a rock. He liked that dark clamshells became swirling mazes of black, gray, and white under the glass.

Thomas's grandmother picked up something from the rocky shore.

"What did you find?" Thomas asked.

She opened her hand. "A piece of sea glass."

"It doesn't look like glass."

Grandmother placed it in Thomas's hand. "Years ago, something made of glass was dropped into the sea, and after being broken and tossed in salt water and sand, the pieces turned smooth and cloudy."

Thomas ran his fingers along the rounded edges, then held the green glass to the morning sun.

"Where do you think it came from?"

"I'm not sure," Grandmother said. "But your grandfather used to say that each piece of sea glass has a story all its own."

That night, with the sea glass on the table beside his bed, Thomas dreamed of a shipyard long ago.

Kellen wiggled through the crowd, hoping for a better view. He and Papa waited at the shipyard for the ceremony to begin.

Over the heads of the people, a huge navy destroyer — a powerful mass of iron and steel, ready for battle, and held together with the sweat and hard work of many craftsmen — rose from the dock.

"Did you really build her, Papa?"

Papa laughed. "Not by myself, son."

"Are you proud?"

"Proud as a man can be."

On the platform, men and ladies dressed as if it were Sunday morning gathered at the bow of the enormous ship.

"What's happening?" Kellen whispered when an elegant woman stepped forward.

"Shh. Mrs. Knox is about to speak," Papa answered, and then placed a finger to his lips.

Kellen stood on his tiptoes just in time to see Mrs. Knox swing a bottle of champagne. "I christen this ship the USS Frank Knox!" she shouted over the cheers of the crowd. And the green glass bottle shattered into a hundred pieces and fell into the water. ⁓

Each morning that summer, Thomas and his grandmother hurried down to the beach to see what the tide had left behind.

Once Thomas found a real treasure: a large chunk of sea glass with a few letters — SON — just barely raised on its surface. Thomas wondered what word the letters might have been a part of and what story this piece of glass might tell.

When Thomas slipped between the cool sheets that night, he dreamed of wind and waves and a terrible storm.

When Thomas slipped between the cool sheets that night, he dreamed of wind and waves and a terrible storm.

The captain's shouted orders could barely be heard over the roar of the wind as men scurried to their stations.

"Lower the sails!"

But the white sails that had once billowed lay in tatters. The mast creaked and groaned against an angry wind.

The schooner listed to starboard, and sailors slid across its flooded deck.

The storm raged, and the brave men fought until they heard the captain's desperate cry: "Abandon ship!"

The captain stayed with his vessel until every last sailor was safe, and then he, too, boarded a lifeboat and headed for shore.

Below the decks of the mighty ship, pots and pans crashed to the galley floor. Shelves of canned wax beans and peaches were toppled, and one Mason jar after another shattered.

When a ferocious wave came up over the bow of the schooner, it took the ship and all its contents to the bottom of the sea.

Throughout that summer, Thomas's favorite days were sea glass days, and his favorite nights were sea glass nights. As the summer days grew slowly shorter, Thomas's grandmother began to prepare the cottage for autumn. And Thomas continued to comb the shore for more of the sea's stories.

One morning, Grandmother said, "We'll leave for the mainland early tomorrow." As an osprey soared overhead, they descended the staircase to the beach one last time. Thomas hoped to find one more piece of sea glass. He hoped to have one last exciting dream.

He searched and searched, but all Thomas found that day were rocks and broken clamshells.

As he lay in bed on that last night, Thomas could smell the salt of the ocean.
He could hear the whisper of the wind. He looked at Grandfather's magnifying
glass on the bedside table. Perhaps he'd dream of his grandfather.

Finally, his eyelids became heavy.

That night Thomas dreamed of . . . nothing.

In the morning, Thomas gathered his favorite summer treasures—a smooth beach rock, two clamshells, Grandfather's magnifying glass, and his precious sea glass—and boarded a ferry.

When the ferry lurched forward, he lost his balance, and Grandfather's magnifying glass slipped from his fingers onto the big boat's wooden deck.

With a heavy heart, Thomas began to pick up what was left of the shattered magnifying glass. Then Grandmother helped him wrap the pieces in his handkerchief.

He stood and watched as the island disappeared from view.

Thomas's sea glass summer was over.

N ot so many years ago, a girl named Annie arrived at her family's cottage by the sea. Annie was a collector of all sorts of treasures. At home she collected acorn cups and pinecones and meadow flowers.

At the seashore, she found different things to collect. She delighted in clamshells and the smoothest rocks. And one day, when Annie was exploring the shallow tide pools near the cottage, she found an unusual piece of sea glass.

"Papaw Tom!" Annie raced to her grandfather's beach chair and placed her new treasure in his hand. "Look what I found!"

Papaw Tom lifted the piece of sea glass to the sun. Its edges were smooth and worn and the once-clear glass was now a cloudy white, but in Papaw Tom's hand, it felt strangely familiar.

"You know, they say each piece of sea glass has a story all its own," he said. "Just imagine what tale this glass could tell."

That night, with her treasures by her side, Annie slept soundly . . .

and dreamed of a boy named Thomas.

AUTHOR'S NOTE

Years ago, before recycling was common, the ocean was considered a good place to discard all kinds of trash. Today, we are more careful about what goes into our waters. While less glass in the ocean is better for the environment, it also means that fewer pieces of colorful sea glass will wash up on the shores, making each piece we find a unique look into the past.